This book is for Niles Harris — J. H. K.

To Robin and Emily — G. C.

Copyright © 1995 Rabbit Ears Productions, Inc., Rowayton, Connecticut

Rabbit Ears Books is an imprint of Rabbit Ears Productions, Inc.

Published by Simon & Schuster, Inc.
1230 Avenue of the Americas
New York, NY 10020

All rights reserved.
Book design by Frezzolini Severance Design
Manufactured in the United States of America
10 9 8 7 6 5 4 3 2 1

Library of Congress Catalog Card Number: 94-68004

ISBN 0-689-80063-0

Aladdin

AND THE MAGIC LAMP

ADAPTED BY
JAMES HOWARD KUNSTLER

ILLUSTRATED BY
GREG COUCH

RABBIT EARS BOOKS

Years ago, at Isfahan in the kingdom of Persia, there lived a boy named Aladdin, the only son of Mustapha, the tailor. Poor Mustapha could barely support his little family, though he toiled like a slave, ever yearning for the day when he and Aladdin might work side by side in the shop. But this was not to be, for Aladdin lived only to loaf around the bazaar, snitching figs from the fruitsellers' stalls, and he showed no interest in learning any useful thing, particularly in his father's trade.

"By the blessed beard of Omar, your idleness will be the death of me!" Aladdin's father would cry. And so it was, for worry and sorrow finally broke Mustapha's heart and his spirit departed this world, leaving his family poorer than ever.

Other boys of fifteen years might be forced by the loss of a father to grow up overnight, but not Aladdin. He wasted more time than ever in childish pranks and idleness until his poor mother threatened to throw him out of the house.

"By the stars and heavens, you are a lazy baboon!" she would say, and then weep for her future.

Now it happened this same year that a mysterious magician from Barbary, Africa, arrived in Isfahan. Seeing Aladdin loafing in the bazaar, he strode up to him and said, "Boy, I am your long-lost uncle. Come and embrace me."

"I never heard of you," Aladdin said.

"Of course not, for I was long-lost," said the magician. "But now we have found each other!"

"Ah, that makes sense," said Aladdin.

"Just so," the magician said.

So Aladdin invited home this stranger who claimed to be his uncle. The magician came with baskets of luscious fruit and meat pies and almond cakes from the bazaar. He bought the youth a fine embroidered suit, gave him two gold ducats a day for pocket money, and promised to set him up in business with a rug merchant's stall in the bazaar. In short, this magician made himself as beloved as a second father to Aladdin.

One fine day, the magician took the boy out of the city in order, he said, to show Aladdin the beauties of the countryside, and how the nobles lived. Indeed, they passed many a splendid estate, and marveled at the palaces and the fragrant gardens with their splashing fountains, and strayed farther until the minarets of Isfahan faded from view, and the muezzins' (*myoo ez´inz*) call to afternoon prayers could no longer be heard, and the country grew wild and rugged. At last they came to a steep ravine between two mountains.

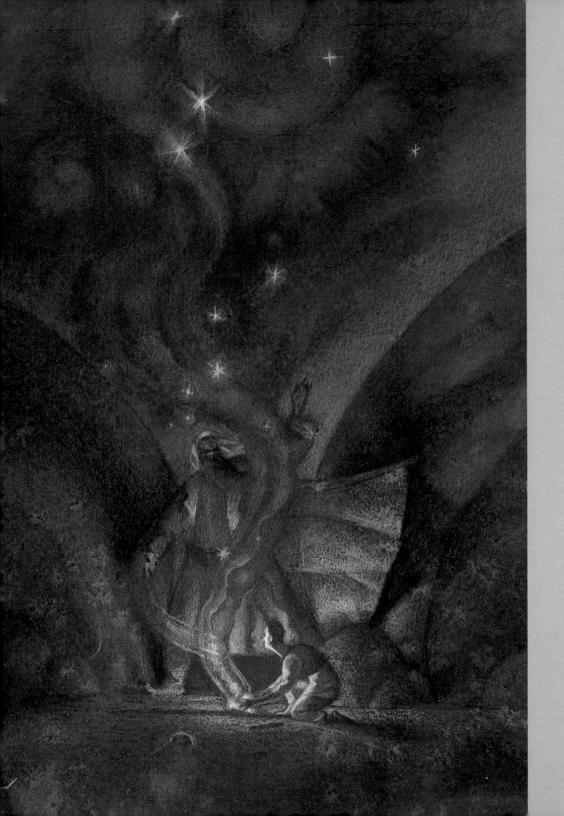

"Make a fire, boy, and I will show you wonders beyond the dreams of a thousand sultans," the magician said. When the flames began to crackle, he flung a fistful of powders from a pouch he carried on his belt while muttering some strange words. The sky darkened, the earth shook, and a colossal boulder rolled aside revealing a cave entrance as dark as the deepest well.

"Climb down in there, Aladdin," he beckoned. "You will pass through three great chambers and a sunken garden where the trees sprout miraculous fruits. Go deeper still. In a niche on the farthest wall of the farthest room you will find an oil lamp. Bring it here to me."

Aladdin glanced fearfully down the hole. "But it's so d-d-dark and s-s-scary," he said. "W-w-why don't you go instead, Uncle?"

"Because it is said there are narrow passageways that only such a slender lad as yourself can squeeze through. Here, take this enchanted ring," the magician said, pulling it off his finger. "I guarantee it will preserve you against all harm. Be bold now, for great fortune awaits us!"

Aladdin crawled down into the cave and hurried through the three gloomy chambers. These led to a fabulous underground garden where silver trees stood, and from their branches hung fruits more dazzling than any Aladdin had ever seen in the bazaar. In fact, these fruits were enormous jewels: red rubies, green emeralds, blue sapphires, creamy pearls, and fiery diamonds. Aladdin had no idea of their value, but they were so pretty that he picked several pounds and stuffed them inside his shirt. Finally, he came to the cave's deepest chamber, grabbed the old brass lamp from its niche, and quickly retraced his steps to the entrance.

"There you are at last!" the magician said, grinning and rubbing his hands. "Good boy!"

"Help me up, Uncle," Aladdin said.

"In a moment. First hand me the lamp, Nephew."

"Dear Uncle, help me up first."

"No, give me the lamp first," the magician insisted, growing annoyed.

"Please, me first, Uncle!" Aladdin begged him.

"The lamp!"

"Me first!"

"Insolent wretch!" the magician howled and he flew into such a rage that the earth shook, and the boulder rolled back into place, sealing Aladdin inside the cave.

Now it can be explained. This magician was nobody's uncle at all but merely an evil schemer. He had selected Aladdin only to help obtain the magic lamp.

Lacking any more magic powders, he was forced to give up his evil quest entirely and return to Barbary, Africa, empty-handed.

Well, this left Aladdin trapped in darkness underground, of course. And idly rubbing the lamp in mortal terror at his predicament, he caused a bright cloud of gas to billow out of its spout, and from this gassy cloud emerged a gigantic, fierce-looking genie.

"W-w-who are you?"

"I am the slave of the lamp, O Master," the genie said, "and your wish is my command."

His mind swimming in fear and wonder, Aladdin blurted out, "Oh, how I wish that I were safe at home!" And the next moment he was magically transported to his own little room in Isfahan. So grateful was he to escape that he swore, "By the stars and heavens, I shall never be an idle baboon or a bad son again!"

In fact, so moderate in his ways did Aladdin become that he would hardly call upon the genie of the lamp, except to bring meals when he and his mother were hungry. He dared not test the genie's greater powers, for he'd seen what kind of trouble magic leads to. And so Aladdin and his mother lived quietly until he reached manhood—when love came along and shook up his world like an earthquake.

It happened this way: Passing by a back wall of the sultan's palace one morning, Aladdin heard squeals of laughter. With innocent curiosity, he peered through a chink in the wall only to see the sultan's beautiful daughter and her handmaidens playing the game of tigers and monkeys in the royal garden. Aladdin watched in thrall as they scampered around the pomegranate trees and splashing fountains.

On the very spot he resolved to marry the princess. "The sight of you," Aladdin murmured to himself, "has made roasted meat of my heart."

Of course such a notion for a common tailor's son was sheer madness. "Marry the sultan's daughter, indeed," his mother gasped. "And be glad that the sultan does not pluck out every hair on your head for such impudence!"

Even so, Aladdin's desire for the princess proved unshakable, though he was as ignorant about the art of courtship as a horse is of astronomy. So, desperately seeking advice, he rubbed the magic lamp until the genie billowed out.

"I am in love with the sultan's daughter," Aladdin said. "What shall I do?"

And the genie said, "Remember those dazzling fruits you picked in the underground garden?"

"Why, yes," said Aladdin, who had kept them at home in a linen sack all these years.

"They are jewels of great value. Bring them to the sultan and ask for the hand of the princess."

Aladdin hastened to the sultan's court. The jewels he presented equaled in worth all the riches of the sultan's treasury. "Am I not worthy of the princess, O great Sultan?" Aladdin asked.

The sultan almost said yes. But his most trusted adviser, the grand vizier, leaned over and whispered, "This fellow looks like a common ragamuffin. Tell him he must bring you four hundred trays of pure gold, laden with all the pearls of China, borne on the back of four hundred slaves, before you will consider his outrageous proposal."

Then he smirked at Aladdin. Aladdin just listened, and smiled to himself as he left the palace.

The next morning, the citizens of Isfahan woke up, startled to see a procession of four hundred slaves marching to the palace, bearing gold trays laden with all the pearls of China.

And to make his intentions perfectly clear, Aladdin followed these by two hundred camels bearing all the perfumes of Araby, and one hundred elephants bearing all the spices of India. Without further ado, the sultan gave away his daughter to be Aladdin's wife. It thrilled the princess to be matched with such a handsome young husband.

Now Aladdin needed a place to live worthy of his new royal bride. Surely he could not bring her home to live in the family's cramped quarters. So Aladdin rubbed the magic lamp and said, "Genie, I command you to build me a home fit for a princess." And overnight a magnificent palace made of jade, alabaster, and onyx sprang up across the square from the sultan's own palace, and here the couple came to dwell in love and happiness.

Now it happened one day that Aladdin went out hunting with the sultan, far from the gates of Isfahan. And by a queer coincidence, there also appeared that day on the streets of the city a beggarly-looking peddler who pulled a cart through the narrow streets of town, crying, "New lamps for old! Who will trade old lamps for new ones?"

"Did you hear that?" remarked the princess to her handmaidens, as they arranged flowers in her glossy black hair.

Now, wishing to do something that would please Aladdin, the princess went to the dressing room, where her husband kept an old tarnished oil lamp, and commanded the peddler to be let inside the palace. With bare feet, tattered robes, and a patch over one eye, this peddler was a most pathetic sight amid all the splendor of the great hall.

"Explain to me, peddler," the princess asked, "how can you make a livelihood out of such a silly business: giving away perfectly good new lamps for useless old ones?"

"I do it for the love of mankind," the peddler answered.

"Well, if it pleases you, you may have this battered old thing," she said.

A smile turned his thin-lipped mouth upward at the corners as his bony hand grasped the ancient lamp. At the same time, a little sigh escaped his throat as though he had finally satisfied a lifelong yearning.

"It seems to give you such pleasure to do this selfless deed," the princess remarked.

"Oh, indeed, Your Highness, nothing is more rewarding than to spread light through this benighted world," he replied. And bidding the princess and her retinue good day, he was heard to cackle with strange glee as the massive jade doors were thrown open for his exit.

Now it can be told. This seemingly selfless peddler was none other than the evil magician of Barbary, Africa, who, years ago, had traveled so far to find the fabled magic lamp of Isfahan — only to lose it to the boy, Aladdin. Since that time, he had pored over secret writings, looked for omens in chicken bones, drawn diabolic figures in the sand, and studied every way he knew to get back the lamp. Now came his sweet moment of triumph.

Skulking down the alley behind Aladdin's palace, the magician threw off his eye-patch and rubbed the old lamp until a cloud billowed forth and the genie appeared. "Ha, ha!" the magician crowed with joy.

"Your wish is my command," the genie said, for he was bound to honor whoever possessed the lamp.

"Pick up Aladdin's palace and all who are in it and transport it to Barbary, Africa!"

And it was done. All had vanished from the spot in Isfahan: the palace with all its gardens, the many slaves and servants, and even the princess herself.

Well now, coming home from the hunt with the sultan, Aladdin was astounded to see that his palace was gone, and with it the love and soul of his life, the princess. The sultan, for his part, was more than astounded — he flew into a towering fury at Aladdin.

"I should have listened to the grand vizier who said that you were a low-born dog!" the sultan howled. "By the beard of Allah himself, I will make you pay!"

And so was Aladdin brought to languish in the deepest and darkest cell of the sultan's dungeons, while the sultan's soldiers searched all over the land for the princess.

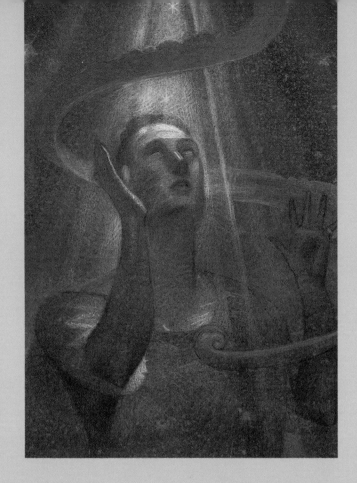

The date was set for Aladdin's execution. Aladdin, for his part, was stoical and resigned until the final hours. But as the fateful moment approached, he began to wring his hands in terror. And so doing, he rubbed the ring that the magician had slipped on his finger so many years ago at the cave entrance. Suddenly, a cloud billowed from the ring and a genie appeared.

"I am the genie of the ring," it said, "and your wish is my command."

"Hurry!" Aladdin cried. "Transport me to my palace at once, wherever it is!" And it was done.

An instant later, he looked about to see all the familiar trappings of his wife's boudoir. And in the next chamber, he could see her seated stiffly on a cushion beside the hated magician, who tried to woo the princess while tears coursed down her cheeks. Aladdin rubbed his ring and the genie appeared again.

"Turn me into a viper for five minutes," he commanded. And it was done. Aladdin slithered across the cold marble tiles into the far chamber.

"There's no use weeping, my little jewel," the magician cooed evilly to the princess. " For now you are all mine, and no power on earth can save you."

The evil wretch bent to kiss the tender skin of her neck, when a viper of the most venomous sort crawled up one leg of his pantaloons and bit him on his hindmost parts. The magician's eyes crossed, smoke curled out his narrow nostrils, and his thin lips babbled wordlessly until he keeled over as dead as a stone.

A moment later, Aladdin
was restored to the body of a
man. And seeing him, the
princess gave a cry of joy to
silence all the muezzins of
Persia.

Aladdin recovered his
magic lamp and before the
sun struck noon, his palace
and everyone in it reappeared
at Isfahan. The sultan
dismissed all charges against
Aladdin, then commanded the
drums, trumpets, and cymbals
to announce his joy to the
public, who began a festival of
ten days to celebrate.

The genie of the lamp was
much pleased to be saved
from such a wicked master as
the evil magician, and served
Aladdin evermore with extra
special diligence.

In a few years, the sultan died in good old age. And the princess and Aladdin inherited his throne. Their reign was a long and happy one and the people of Isfahan enjoyed many, many blessings.